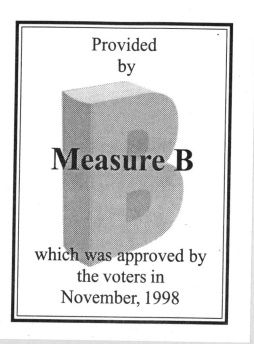

For Pete's Sake

ELLEN STOLL WALSH

HARCOURT BRACE & COMPANY

San Diego   New York   London

Requests for permission to make copies of any part of the work
should be mailed to: Permissions Department, Harcourt Brace & Company,
6277 Sea Harbor Drive, Orlando, Florida 32887-6777.

Library of Congress Cataloging-in-Publication Data
Walsh, Ellen Stoll.
For Pete's sake/Ellen Stoll Walsh.
p. cm.
Summary: Pete, an alligator who thinks that he is a flamingo,
worries when he begins to notice the differences between him
and his flamingo friends.
ISBN 0-15-200324-X
[1. Alligators—Fiction. 2. Flamingos—Fiction. 3. Individuality—Fiction.] I. Title.
PZ7.W1675Fo 1998
[E]—dc21   97-25677

F E D C

Printed in Singapore

For my sister Mink

"I'm green," said Pete. "I want to be pink. Everyone else is."

"Don't worry," said the others.
"You probably aren't ripe yet.
It takes longer for some."

"Is that true?" Pete wondered.

"Probably," they said. "Let's play in the sand!"

"Oh no," cried Pete. "I have four feet.
No one else has four feet."

"You're lucky, Pete," said the others. "Two, and two extra. C'mon. Let's go wading."

Pete tried to feel lucky.
Before long he was having fun.

"Stop!" said the others, laughing.

"You're getting our feathers wet."

Uh-oh. Pete didn't have any feathers.

"The best feathers take the longest to grow,"
they said. "Hurry, it's getting late."

The others hurried home.

But poor, green, featherless Pete
poked along on his four feet...

...very, very slowly.

Nothing could cheer him up.

Then one day some strangers stopped
by on their way to the swamp. Flamingos
who looked just like Pete.

Pete almost popped with joy.

"I'm different but the same,"
he told the others.

"Well for Pete's sake, Pete," they said.
"You always have been."

The illustrations in this book are cut-paper collage.
The display and text type were set in OptiSusan.
Color separations were made by Tien Wah Press, Singapore.
Printed and bound by Tien Wah Press, Singapore
This book was printed on totally chlorine-free Nymolla Matte Art paper.
Production supervision by Stanley Redfern
Designed by Judythe Sieck